P9-DGH-891

PELHAM SCHOOL DISTRICT
PELHAM, N. H.

E.G. Sherburne School

GREENLAND
CANADA
VERMONT
U. S. A.
JAMAICA
ATLANTIC OCEAN
PACIFIC OCEAN
SOUTH
AMERICA

BERING SEA
RUSSIA
LY
CHINA
JAPAN
INDIA
ICA
SRI LANKA
INDIAN OCEAN
THE WORLD
AUSTRALIA

How to Make an Apple Pie and see the world

E.G. Sherburne School

by Marjorie Priceman

Dragonfly Books™
Alfred A. Knopf • New York

7/01
Perma-
Bound
12.14

DRAGONFLY BOOKS™ PUBLISHED BY ALFRED A. KNOPF, INC.
Copyright © 1994 by Marjorie Priceman

All rights reserved under International and Pan-American
Copyright Conventions. Published in the United States of America by Alfred A. Knopf, Inc.,
New York, and simultaneously in Canada by Random House of Canada Limited, Toronto.
Distributed by Random House, Inc., New York. Originally published in hardcover as a
Borzoi Book by Alfred A. Knopf, Inc., in 1994.

Library of Congress Cataloging-in-Publication Data
Priceman, Marjorie.
How to make an apple pie and see the world / by Marjorie Priceman.
p. cm.
Summary: Since the market is closed, the reader is led around the world to gather
the ingredients for making an apple pie.
ISBN 0-679-83705-1 (trade) — ISBN 0-679-93705-6 (lib. bdg.)
ISBN 0-679-88083-6 (pbk.)

[1. Pies—Fiction. 2. Food—Fiction. 3. Voyages and travels—Fiction.
4. Humorous stories.] I. Title
PZ7.P932Ho 1994 [E]—dc20 93-12341

First Dragonfly Books™ edition: September 1996
Printed in the United States of America
10 9 8 7

http://www.randomhouse.com/

_M_aking an apple pie is really very easy.
First, get all the ingredients at the market.
Mix them well, bake, and serve.

Unless, of course,
the market is closed.

In that case, go home and pack a suitcase. Take your shopping list and some walking shoes. Then catch a steamship bound for Europe. Use the six days on board to brush up on your Italian.

If you time it right, you'll arrive in Italy at harvest time.
Find a farm deep in the countryside. Gather some
superb semolina wheat. An armful or two will do.

Then hop a train to France
and locate a chicken.

French chickens lay elegant eggs—and you want only
the finest ingredients for your pie. Coax the chicken to
give you an egg. Better yet, bring the chicken with you.
There's less chance of breaking the egg that way.

Get to Sri Lanka any way you can.

You can't miss it. Sri Lanka is a pear-shaped island in the Indian Ocean. The best cinnamon in the world is made there, from the bark of the native kurundu tree. So go directly to the rain forest. Find a kurundu tree and peel off some bark. If a leopard is napping beneath the tree, be very quiet.

Hitch a ride to England. Make the acquaintance of a cow. You'll know she's an English cow from her good manners and charming accent. Ask if you can borrow a cup or two of milk. Even better, bring the whole cow with you for the freshest possible results.

Stow away on a banana boat headed home to Jamaica.
On your way there, you can pick up some salt. Fill a
jar with salty seawater.

When the boat docks in Jamaica, walk to the nearest sugar plantation. Introduce yourself to everyone. Tell them about the pie you're making. Then go into the fields and cut a few stalks of sugar cane.

Better fly home. You don't want the ingredients to spoil.

Wait a minute. Aren't you forgetting something?
WHAT ABOUT THE APPLES? Have the pilot
drop you off in Vermont.

You won't have to go far to find an apple orchard. Pick eight rosy apples from the top of the tree. Give one to the chicken, one to the cow, and eat one yourself. That leaves five for the pie. Then hurry home.

Now all you have to do is
mill the wheat into flour,

grind the kurundu
bark into cinnamon,

evaporate the seawater
from the salt,

boil the sugar cane,

persuade the chicken
to lay an egg,

milk the cow,

churn the milk
into butter,

slice the apples,

mix the ingredients,
and bake the pie.

While the pie is cooling, invite some
friends over to share it with you.

Remember that apple pie is delicious topped with
vanilla ice cream, which you can get at the market.
But if the market happens to be closed . . .

YOU CAN EAT IT PLAIN!

Apple Pie

CRUST

2 cups flour

1 teaspoon salt

1 cup butter

½ cup ice water

1 egg yolk

Sift flour and salt together in a bowl. Quickly rub small pieces of cold butter into the flour mixture with your fingers until bits are the size of peas. Add ice water, starting with a few tablespoons and adding more as needed to moisten all the dough. Stir with a fork until mixture forms a loose ball. Divide dough in half and make two equal patties. Place one patty between two pieces of wax paper . With a rolling pin or bottle, roll into a 12-inch circle. Peel off the top piece of wax paper and turn into pie pan. Remove wax paper. Trim around the edge. Roll out the top crust in the same way. Refrigerate both until ready to use.

FILLING

5–7 apples

¾ cup sugar

1 teaspoon cinnamon

¼ teaspoon salt

2 tablespoons butter

Preheat oven to 425°. In a large bowl, mix together sugar, cinnamon, and salt. Peel, core, and cut apples into ½-inch slices. Toss the apples into the sugar mixture, coating them well. Arrange apple slices in the pie pan, piling them higher in the center. Dot with butter. Moisten the edge of the bottom crust with water. Cover the pie with the top crust, trim the edge, then pinch top and bottom edges together. Cut some vents in the top crust. To glaze the crust, mix an egg yolk with 1 tablespoon of water. Brush the mixture over the surface of the top crust. Bake 45 minutes or until apples are tender and crust is golden brown. Remove pie and allow to cool before serving.

GREENLAND

CANADA

EH

VERMONT

U. S. A.

ATLANTIC OCEAN

JAMAICA

PACIFIC OCEAN

SOUTH

AMERICA

BERING SEA

RUSSIA

LY

CHINA

JAPAN

INDIA

ICA

SRI LANKA

INDIAN OCEAN

THE WORLD

AUSTRALIA

PROPERTY OF
PELHAM SCHOOL DISTRICT
PELHAM, N. H.

E.G. Sherburne School